I0530572

A Heart

Worth

Mending

A Small-Town, Age-Gap Romance Between a Grumpy Vet and the Sunshine Baker Who Helped Heal His Heart

Hana York

Pink Pop Publishing

A Heart Worth Mending

(Hearts on Duty Book 6)

Copyright © 2025 by Hana York

All rights reserved.

No portion of this book may be reproduced in any form without written permission from the publisher or author, except as permitted by U.S. copyright law.

www.HanaYork.com

Contents

Chapter One

♥

PENELOPE

The glass door of Milo's clinic swung open with a sharp jingle as I rushed inside, cradling the tiny bundle of russet fur against my chest.

"Milo!" I called, not bothering with pleasantries. "I need your help—this fox is hurt. He's limping, and I think his leg might be broken."

Milo Turner, resident grump, and Anchor Bay's most reluctant hero, barely looked up from whatever Very Important Paperwork he was pretending to be focused on.

His sigh was slow, long-suffering. "Tell me you didn't bring another wild animal into my clinic."

I blew a rogue curl out of my face, barely fazed by his tone. My messy bun—if you could still call it that—had given up entirely somewhere between the bakery and here, stray tendrils escaping in all directions like they had somewhere better to be. No matter how much I tried to tame it, it had a mind of its own, like everything else in my life.

I adjusted my grip on the fox and shot Milo a look. "What was I supposed to do? Leave him there?"

His arms crossed over his chest, his eyes flat. "Wildlife Services exist for a reason, Penelope."

"They're not you," I shot back, knowing I'd won this round. "And you were closer."

His jaw twitched, but his gaze finally flicked to the fox. I could see the exact second his instincts kicked in. Without another word, he jerked his head toward the desk. "Bring him over."

I hurried forward, setting the fox down gently as Milo started his examination, his hands steady and sure.

"I think his leg's broken," I repeated, watching his face for any flicker of concern. "He was limping when I found him."

Milo barely glanced at me as he ran his fingers over the fox's leg. "Sprained, not broken," he muttered. "And you really have to stop bringing me every injured animal in a five-mile radius."

"It was hurt," I argued, hands on my hips. "What was I supposed to do? Walk away?"

"Yes," Milo said dryly. "That's typically an option."

I scoffed. "Not for me."

His sigh this time was different—less annoyed, more resigned. "Yeah, I know."

The tension in my shoulders eased. "So, you'll fix him?"

His fingers stilled for half a second before he shook his head, muttering under his breath. "Yeah, I'll fix him."

"I knew you would," I said brightly.

Milo didn't even look up. "Of course you did."

I grinned, rocking back on my heels as I watched him work. The fox let out a small, weak yip, and I instinctively stroked its fur.

Milo's voice broke the quiet. "Why do you always do that?"

"Do what?"

"Act like it's a given that I'll help." His tone was unreadable, and he still wasn't looking at me.

I studied him for a second. "Because it is."

His lips pressed into a flat line.

I leaned in slightly. "Grumpy as you are, you've got a heart of gold under all that brooding."

Milo snorted, finishing the wrap on the fox's leg. "You're lucky I like animals more than people."

I grinned. "Is that your way of saying I'm not your favorite person?"

This time, he did glance up, his gaze sharp. "It's my way of saying you're impossible."

I took that as a win.

Milo placed a hand gently on the fox's side, checking the bandage one last time before straightening. "I'll keep him here for observation overnight and then he'll go to Wildlife Services for rehab."

"You're the best, Milo!"

His expression didn't change, but I caught the faintest twitch at the corner of his mouth before he turned back to the fox.

MILO

As Penelope walked out, the room didn't feel any calmer. If anything, it felt like she'd left some of her energy behind, still buzzing in the air.

I exhaled, rubbing a hand down my face before glancing at the fox. It stared up at me, wide-eyed, like it had something to say.

"What?" I muttered. "Don't look at me like that. You know she's impossible."

The fox blinked.

I sighed, shaking my head. "Yeah, I know. I'm screwed."

The fox made a sound that could've been an agreement if foxes understood the concept of a man being completely, utterly out of his depth when it came to five-foot-nothing bakers with wild hair and a wilder heart.

"Don't start," I warned, rechecking the bandage. "She's a walking disaster with a hero complex."

I carried the injured animal to the recovery area in the back, where a row of kennels lined the wall. Most were empty—small miracles—except for Mrs. Barlow's ancient tabby recovering from dental surgery and a beagle with a cone of shame who'd gotten into something he shouldn't have.

I settled the fox into a clean kennel with fresh bedding, filled a small water dish, and ensured he was comfortable. His russet fur reminded me of Penelope's unruly curls, which was precisely the kind of thought I needed to shut down immediately.

I turned away, busying myself with cleaning up the exam area, but my thoughts circled back to Penelope. She'd blown into my life a year ago when she bought the old Willoughby place on Main Street and turned it into Sweet Somethings Bakery. Within a week, half the town was addicted to her lemon blueberry scones, and within a month, she'd somehow appointed herself my personal tormentor.

The fox whimpered, drawing my attention back.

"You're staying overnight," I told him firmly. "Then I'm handing you over to Wildlife Services, where you belong."

The fox yawned, looking thoroughly unimpressed with my declaration.

I grabbed the chart hanging from the wall and started making notes, my pen scratching against the paper. "Patient: wild fox. Treatment: bandaged right leg. Prescribed rest and..." I paused, tapping the pen against my chin, "...distance from overly enthusiastic bakers."

My phone buzzed in my pocket. I didn't need to check it to know who it was.

Penelope: *Is the little guy doing okay?*

I stared at the screen, fighting a smile despite myself.

Me: *He's fine. Resting.*

Three dots appeared immediately, followed by:

Penelope: *I named him Rusty! Do you think he likes blueberries? I could bring some tomorrow on my way into the bakery.*

I sighed, staring at my phone. Of course, she'd named the fox already.

Me: *He's a wild animal, not a pet. And no, don't bring blueberries.*

Her response came instantly:

Penelope: *Spoilsport. I'll bring you a scone instead. The cinnamon ones you pretend not to like but always eat anyway.*

I found myself smiling despite my best efforts. She'd noticed that?

Me: *I eat them to be polite.*

Penelope: *Sure, Doc. Whatever helps you sleep at night. See you at 7!*

I turned away from my phone, trying to ignore the warmth that had settled in my chest. That was the thing about Penelope Everett—she had a way of worming past your defenses before you even realized they were down. Maybe it was how she breezed through life with that permanent smile like she knew something the rest of us didn't. Or perhaps it was how she collected strays—the four-legged kind and the human variety—with the same easy compassion.

"She's bringing scones tomorrow," I told the fox, who was watching me with what looked suspiciously like amusement. "Don't get too attached. To her or the scones."

The fox tilted his head as if to say, "You're one to talk."

"It's professional courtesy," I muttered, more to myself than the animal. "That's all."

But I knew I was lying to myself even as I said it.

Chapter Two

♥

PENELOPE

The goat was winning.

I brandished a baking tray like a shield, my flour-dusted apron swishing as I tried—*in vain*—to herd the four-legged menace away from my display case. "Shoo! You are absolutely not supposed to be here!"

Unimpressed with my authority, the goat stared at me for a long, unbothered second before knocking over an entire tray of scones with a casual flick of its tail.

"Oh, *come on!*" I groaned, dragging a hand through my hair—only to realize too late that it was still covered in flour. Perfect. Now I looked as unhinged as I felt.

I yanked my phone from my pocket, scrolling frantically for the number I didn't want to call.

Milo picked up almost instantly, his voice already wary. "What now, Penelope?"

"I have a situation," I said quickly. "A big one."

A long pause. "Do I even *want* to know?"

I squeezed my eyes shut. "There's a goat in the bakery."

Another pause.

"A goat?"

"Yes, Milo. A goat. A real, live, four-legged menace currently destroying my livelihood!" I glared at the animal, but it ignored me, too busy munching on a fallen croissant.

Milo let out the longest, most put-upon sigh I'd ever heard. "I'll be there in five."

The line went dead.

I shoved my phone into my pocket and turned back to the culprit. "I hope you know you're about to meet the least fun person on the planet."

The goat flicked its tail. If anything, it looked intrigued.

The cavalry—such as it was—arrived two minutes later.

The bell above the door jingled, and Milo strode in, boots heavy against the wood. He stopped just inside, taking in the scene with a slow, exhausted sweep of his eyes.

Flour dust hung in the air. Croissants and scones were scattered across the floor like the aftermath of a battle. And the goat—still perched atop an overturned tray—was working its way through my last blueberry muffin.

The goat flicked its tail like a performer taking the stage—clearly delighted to have a larger audience for its destruction.

"Alright, buddy," Milo murmured, approaching the goat with slow, measured steps. "You're making quite the mess here, you know that?"

The goat eyed Milo with what I could only describe as calculated defiance. I'd never seen an animal look so smug.

"I think it's mocking you," I whispered, peering around Milo's broad shoulders.

He shot me a look. "Not helping, Penelope."

I raised my hands in surrender and backed away, giving him space to work his animal-whispering magic. For all my teasing, I couldn't deny that Milo had a way with creatures that bordered on supernatural. Even the most skittish animals seemed to settle under his calm, steady presence.

The goat, however, was the exception.

As Milo inched closer, the creature suddenly leaped from its perch, darted through Milo's legs and made a beeline for my kitchen.

"No!" I shrieked, diving after it. "Not the kitchen! I just finished the wedding cake for the Hendersons!"

The goat bleated triumphantly, skidding across my pristine floor like it was on a mission. I lunged forward, nearly colliding with Milo as we scrambled to intercept the goat before it reached my masterpiece, sitting vulnerably on the counter.

"Cut it off!" Milo barked, veering right while I went left.

I snatched a rolling pin from the counter—not as a weapon, just for moral support—as I slid in front of the three-tiered confection I'd spent the better part of yesterday perfecting.

"Don't you dare," I warned, voice dropping to a dangerous whisper.

The goat's head turned toward me, and I swear it smiled.

Milo moved with a swiftness I'd never seen before, scooping the animal up in one fluid motion, his arms wrapping securely around its middle as it kicked and squirmed.

"Gotcha," he ground out, voice strained as he struggled to keep his grip. The goat bleated indignantly, hooves flailing.

I sagged against the counter in relief. "My hero," I breathed, only half-joking.

Milo's eyes met mine over the goat's head, and for a split second, something passed between us—a flicker of warmth that made my chest tighten.

Then the goat headbutted him under his chin.

"Son of a—" Milo bit back the curse, adjusting his grip. "Whose goat is this, anyway?"

I shrugged, setting down my rolling pin. "No clue. I was opening up, and it just wandered in when I unlocked the door."

Milo fought to keep his hold on the squirming animal. "Only you, Penelope. Only you would open your door and have a random goat walk in."

"What's that supposed to mean?" I asked, crossing my arms over my flour-dusted apron.

"It means," he grunted as the goat tried to twist free, "that chaos follows you like a shadow."

I couldn't argue with that assessment. My life had always been a series of unexpected detours and happy accidents. It was how I'd ended up in Anchor Bay in the first place—a wrong turn, a flat tire, and a sunset over the harbor that had stolen my heart.

"You make it sound like a bad thing," I said, grabbing a dish towel to wipe flour from my face.

"I think this troublemaker belongs to Old Man Jenkins," Milo said, nodding toward a faded collar I hadn't noticed before. "He's got that small farm on the edge of town."

The goat had finally settled in Milo's arms, seemingly resigned to its capture. Or maybe it was just plotting its next move. Those eyes looked suspiciously calculating.

"I'll take him back after I drop by the clinic," Milo said, adjusting his grip. "Jenkins needs a better fence."

"Wait," I called, hurrying after him. "What about Rusty? Is he okay?"

Milo paused at the door, the goat tucked securely under his arm. "The fox is fine. Ate some chicken I left out for him this morning."

I brightened immediately. "So he has an appetite! That's good, right?"

"It means he's not dying," Milo replied dryly. "Don't get attached, Penelope. He's going to Wildlife Services later today."

"But his leg—"

"Will heal just fine under their care." His tone left no room for argument.

I followed him outside, ignoring the curious stares from early morning passersby.

MILO

The goat finally settled in the back of my truck, secured in a large crate I kept for this kind of emergency. Though, to be fair, "goat invades local bakery" was a new one even for me.

I shut the tailgate more forcefully than necessary, turning to find Penelope still hovering nearby, absently brushing flour from her apron. There was a smudge of it across her cheek that she'd missed, and I had to fight the inexplicable urge to reach out and wipe it away.

"You've got..." I gestured vaguely at my own face.

She immediately swiped at the wrong cheek. "Did I get it?"

"No, it's—" I sighed, giving in to impulse and reaching out to brush the flour from her skin with my thumb. "There."

Penelope went very still under my touch, her eyes widening slightly.

For a moment, time seemed to suspend itself. The early morning bustle of Anchor Bay faded to a distant hum as my hand lingered against her cheek, the warmth of her skin seeping into my fingertips. I should have pulled away. Should have made some gruff comment about how she attracted disaster like flowers attracted bees. Should have climbed into my truck and driven away with the trouble-making goat.

I did none of those things.

Instead, I found myself caught in the amber flecks of her eyes, noticing how they caught the morning sunlight filtering through the maple trees lining Main Street. Had they always been that particular shade of hazel? A color that shifted between forest green and warm honey depending on how the light hit them?

"Milo?" Her voice was soft, questioning, a barely-there whisper that somehow cut through everything else.

The morning sun caught in her wild curls, turning them to burnished copper and gold. Even covered in flour and disheveled from her battle with the goat, she was beautiful in a way that made my chest ache.

The spell broke when the goat let out an impatient bleat from the back of my truck. I dropped my hand like I'd been burned, taking a step back for good measure.

"You should probably clean up before your customers arrive," I said, my voice rough.

Penelope blinked, a flush creeping up her neck. "Right. Yes. The bakery." She gestured vaguely behind her, seeming as off-balance as I felt. "It looks like a flour bomb went off in there."

"Sorry about your scones," I said, glancing at the bakery's open door where the evidence of the morning's chaos was still visible.

Penelope's smile returned, sunshine breaking through clouds. "I'll just make more. Besides, it's a great story to tell my customers. 'Sorry we're opening late—there was a goat situation'."

"Good luck with that," I said, already retreating to the driver's side of my truck. "I'll handle the goat."

"Thanks for the save," she called after me, the familiar teasing note returning to her voice. But something was different this time—a slight tremor, a new awareness that hung between us.

As I pulled away from the curb, I could still see Penelope in my rearview mirror, standing in front of her bakery with that impossible smile, the kind that seemed to suggest the universe was a fundamentally good place. My hand tingled where I'd touched her cheek, and I flexed my fingers against the steering wheel, trying to dispel the sensation.

The goat bleated from the back, a sound so indignant it might have been funny if my thoughts weren't suddenly a tangled mess.

I drove through town on autopilot, barely registering the familiar storefronts and faces. Mrs. Dalloway waved from outside her flower shop. Tom Hollis was sweeping the sidewalk in front of the hardware store. Regular, everyday Anchor Bay—the quiet coastal town that had become my refuge after everything fell apart.

But my mind was still back at Sweet Somethings, caught in that moment when something had shifted between us—a tectonic plate moving beneath the careful foundation I'd built.

The softness of her skin beneath my thumb. The way her eyes had widened. The subtle intake of breath neither of us had acknowledged.

"Damn it," I muttered, tightening my grip on the steering wheel.

The goat bleated again as if in judgment.

"Nobody asked you," I told it, glancing in the rearview mirror.

I pulled up to the clinic but didn't immediately get out. The goat had finally quieted down, probably busy plotting its next invasion. I rested my forehead against the steering wheel, exhaling slowly.

This thing with Penelope—this pull I felt whenever she was around—had to stop. I needed to reinforce the boundaries I'd been letting slip.

I forced myself out of the truck, walking around to retrieve the four-legged menace. The goat eyed me with what looked suspiciously like smugness as I opened the crate.

"You're enjoying this, aren't you?" I muttered, hoisting the animal into my arms. It bleated softly against my chest, suddenly docile.

My assistant, Tara, looked up from the reception desk as I shouldered through the door, her eyebrows climbing toward her hairline.

"Is that—"

"Don't ask," I cut her off. "I'll be in exam room two. Then I need to return this troublemaker to Jenkins."

She nodded, wisely keeping any comments to herself as I carried the goat through to the back.

Twenty minutes later, after confirming the goat was unharmed despite its bakery rampage, I found myself driving down the winding coastal road toward Jenkins' farm. The goat had fallen suspiciously quiet as if it knew exactly where we were headed.

As I drove, my mind circled back to Penelope. I'd been fighting this... whatever it was... since she'd blown into town like a hurricane last year. At first, I'd convinced myself it was just irritation. She was too cheerful, too impulsive, too everything. The complete opposite of the carefully controlled life I'd built for myself after walking away from the military and everything it had cost me.

But irritation didn't explain how my pulse kicked up whenever she burst through my clinic door with some new emergency. Or how I found myself looking for her wild curls in every crowd. Or how I'd memorized her schedule—Mondays, she closed early to teach a baking class at the community center; Thursdays, she stayed late to prep for weekend orders; and Sundays, she walked along the pier at sunrise before opening the bakery.

I knew all this because I'd been watching. Not in a creepy way—at least, I hoped not—but in the way you can't help noticing the brightest light in every room.

The goat bleated softly as I turned onto the gravel drive leading to Jenkins' place, the sound pulling me from thoughts I had no business entertaining.

"Almost home, troublemaker," I muttered, more to distract myself than anything.

Jenkins was already out front when I pulled up, his weathered face creasing into a grin when he spotted his escapee in the back of my truck.

"There's the little devil!" he called, ambling over with the unhurried gait of a man who'd lived through enough to know rushing rarely helped anything. "Figured he'd turn up sooner or later."

I climbed out, shutting the door with more force than necessary. "Your 'little devil' ransacked Sweet Somethings this morning. Nearly took out a wedding cake."

Jenkins chuckled, the sound as rough as the stubble covering his chin. "That sounds like Houdini. Always had a sweet tooth, that one."

"Houdini?" I raised an eyebrow as I opened the crate. The goat trotted out with an air of casual indifference as if being returned home after a morning of bakery destruction was all part of its plan.

"Named him that 'cause he's always escaping," Jenkins explained, scratching the goat behind its ears. "No fence can hold him when he sets his mind to wandering."

I crossed my arms. "Well, you might want to try harder. Miss Everett wasn't thrilled about having her morning inventory turned into Houdini's breakfast."

"Ah, that pretty baker with the wild hair?" Jenkins' eyes twinkled knowingly. "Bet you rushed right over to save the day, didn't you, Doc?"

Heat crept up my neck. "I was called about an animal situation. That's my job."

"Sure, sure." Jenkins nodded, his smile suggesting he wasn't buying my professional detachment for a second.

"I'll make it right with Miss Everett," he promised, leading Houdini toward the barn. "Maybe drop off some of my wife's honey as payment for the damages. Though," he added with a glance over his shoulder, "I reckon she didn't mind the rescue too much, not when it was you doing the rescuing."

I felt my jaw tighten. "Just fix your fence, Jenkins."

The old man's laugh followed me back to my truck. "You know, Doc," he called as I opened the driver's side door, "for a smart man, you can be mighty slow about some things."

I didn't dignify that with a response; I just climbed into my truck and drove away, gravel crunching under the tires. The morning sun was up, painting the coastal road in warm gold as I returned to town.

Chapter Three

♥

MILO

I took the long way back, driving along the coast where the road curved with the shoreline. The water glittered under the morning sun, a deep sapphire blue that made Anchor Bay famous.

When I finally pulled into the clinic parking lot, Tara was waiting for me with a knowing smile that made me immediately suspicious.

"What?" I asked, climbing out of the truck.

She held up a white paper bag with the Sweet Somethings logo stamped on the front. "Delivery from the bakery. Penelope's assistant dropped these off. Said something about 'combat pay for goat wrangling'."

I took the bag, catching the unmistakable scent of cinnamon. Inside were two perfectly baked scones—the ones Penelope knew I couldn't resist despite my protests to the contrary.

"She also left this," Tara added, holding a folded note.

I hesitated before taking it, acutely aware of my assistant's curious gaze. The note was written on Sweet Somethings stationery, Penelope's looping handwriting instantly recognizable.

> *Thanks for saving the bakery (and the Henderson wedding cake) from certain goat destruction. Please accept these as a small token of my appreciation. Can I treat you to dinner tonight? - P*

> *P.S. Rusty needs blueberries. I can tell.*

I found myself smiling before I could stop it, quickly folding the note and shoving it into my pocket when I caught Tara watching me with undisguised interest.

"Not a word," I warned, heading toward the back where the recovery kennels were located.

"Didn't say a thing," Tara called after me, her tone too innocent to be trusted.

The fox—Rusty, as Penelope had insisted on calling him—was awake and alert when I entered the recovery area. His amber eyes followed me as I approached his kennel, ears perked forward with interest.

"Morning," I greeted him, crouching to check his bandaged leg. "Let's see how you're doing today."

The fox allowed me to examine him without protest, which was unusual for a wild animal. Most would be frantic in captivity, but this one seemed almost... patient. Like he understood I was trying to help.

"Your leg's looking better," I told him, gently rewrapping the bandage. "Should be good as new in no time."

The fox blinked slowly, his russet fur catching the light from the window.

"Wildlife Services will take good care of you," I said quietly, more to convince myself than the fox. "They'll release you somewhere safe, away from roads and..." I paused, thinking of flour-dusted cheeks and wild copper curls. "Away from overly enthusiastic bakers who name everything they find."

The fox tilted his head as if questioning my logic.

I straightened up, Penelope's note burning a hole in my pocket. Dinner. Such a simple word for something that felt anything but simple. The logical part of my brain—the part that had kept me safe, kept me distant, kept me from getting hurt (and hurting) again—was already listing all the reasons this was a terrible idea.

The fox's knowing gaze followed me as I paced the kennel area. I ran a hand through my hair, feeling the threads of gray at my temples—a stark reminder of the decade and change I had on Penelope. At thirty-eight, I'd already lived several lifetimes: the eager young veterinary student, the battle-hardened Army vet who'd patched up military working dogs in Afghanistan, and now the small-town animal doctor trying to outrun ghosts that still woke me at 3 am.

"She's twenty-six," I muttered to the fox. "Twenty-six."

Rusty cocked his head, his expression questioning.

"Don't look at me like that," I said, checking his water bowl for the third time. "You don't understand what's at stake."

The truth was, Penelope Everett was sunshine personified.

She made friends with strangers in grocery store lines, remembered everyone's birthday, and left surprise pastries on doorsteps "just because." And for reasons I couldn't comprehend, she'd decided I belonged in her orbit.

The fox yipped softly, drawing my attention back.

"It's not that simple," I told him, leaning against the counter. "I'm not what she thinks I am."

But even as I said it, I was reaching for my phone, thumbing open my messages before I could talk myself out of it.

Me: *Thanks for the scones. Dinner sounds good. 7 pm?*

I hit send before I could change my mind. The fox watched the entire process with what looked suspiciously like amusement.

"Not a word," I told him, pointing a finger at his furry face. "You're supposed to be on my side."

My phone buzzed almost immediately. I tried to ignore how my stomach flipped as I checked my phone.

Penelope: *Perfect! Meet at my place? I'll cook Unless you want to go out? We could do Malone's Or that new place on the pier? Your choice!*

I could practically hear her rapid-fire delivery and see the animated way her hands would gesture as she talked. A smile tugged at my lips before I could stop it.

Me: *Your place is fine. I'll bring wine.*

Her response was instantaneous:

Penelope: *Red, please! Can't wait!*

I typed back a quick affirmative, ignoring how my pulse kicked up. It was ridiculous. I was a grown man, not some teenager going to prom. This was just dinner with... a friend? Was that what Penelope was to me?

The fox yipped again, drawing my attention.

"This doesn't concern you," I informed him, pocketing my phone.

PENELOPE

"It's not a date," I told my reflection firmly, trying to tame a particularly stubborn curl that refused to cooperate. "Just dinner. With a friend. A grumpy, ridiculously handsome friend who saved my bakery from goat destruction."

My reflection didn't seem convinced. Neither was I, if I was being honest.

I'd spent the afternoon in a state of barely contained nervous energy, cleaning my already clean apartment above the bakery, then stress-baking three different desserts before finally settling on a simple but elegant menu: rosemary garlic chicken, roasted vegetables, fresh bread I'd made that morning, and lemon mousse with blackberry compote for dessert.

Nothing fancy. Nothing that screamed, "I've been thinking about you constantly since you touched my face this morning."

I groaned, dropping my forehead against the cool mirror. "Get it together, Penelope."

The truth was, I'd been drawn to Milo Turner from the moment I'd barged into his clinic a year ago, carrying a bedraggled seagull with a broken wing I'd found on the beach during my morning walk. He'd been gruff, exasperated, and utterly competent as he'd examined the bird, his hands gentle despite his brusque demeanor.

I'd been fascinated by the contradiction—the tough exterior that couldn't entirely hide the care he took with every creature that crossed his path.

Over the past year, I'd made it my mission to crack through the carefully constructed wall he kept between himself and the rest of the world. Not because I enjoyed annoying him (though I did), but because something told me the real Milo Turner was worth knowing.

I straightened up, giving my reflection one last critical look. I'd opted for casual—jeans and a soft green sweater. The sweater brought out the green in my hazel eyes and complemented my copper curls, which I'd finally managed to somewhat tame. Not too dressy, but nice enough to show I'd made an effort.

"It's not a date," I repeated, even as the flutter in my stomach suggested otherwise.

The timer on my phone chimed, reminding me to check on the chicken. I hurried to the kitchen, the hardwood floors cool beneath my bare feet. My apartment wasn't large, but it was mine—a cozy space with exposed brick walls and large windows that overlooked Main Street. The bakery took up the entire ground floor, and I'd converted the upstairs into a home that reflected the organized chaos of my life: colorful throw pillows, mismatched vintage furniture, and plants in every corner.

I was basting the chicken when a knock sounded at my door, sending my heart lurching into my throat. It was precisely 7 pm because, of course, Milo would be exactly on time. Not early (presumptuous), not late (disrespectful).

I took a deep breath and ran my fingers through my curls. When I pulled open the door, my breath caught. Milo stood on the threshold, a bottle of wine in one hand and—unexpectedly—a small bouquet of wildflowers in the other. He'd changed from his usual clinic attire into dark jeans and a navy button-down, making his eyes look even more intensely blue.

"Hi," I said, suddenly feeling shy despite myself.

Milo shifted slightly, looking almost uncertain. "Hi." His eyes flickered over me briefly before returning to my face. "These are for you." He extended the wildflowers, a collection of black-eyed Susans, Queen Anne's lace, and something purple I couldn't identify.

I took the flowers, trying to hide my smile. The fact that Milo had picked wildflowers for me sent a warm flutter through my chest.

"They're beautiful," I said, stepping back to let him in. "Come in. Dinner's almost ready."

Milo stepped inside, his tall frame making my apartment feel smaller somehow. As he passed, I caught a hint of his scent—clean soap and something woodsy. He moved with that careful precision I'd noticed before, like a man constantly aware of the space he occupied.

"Something smells amazing," he said, glancing toward the kitchen where steam rose from the oven. "I didn't know you could cook beyond pastries."

I laughed, moving to find a vase for the flowers. "There's a lot you don't know about me, Dr. Turner."

"Apparently," he murmured, eyes following me as I filled a mason jar with water and arranged the wildflowers. "I wasn't sure what to bring, so..." He held up the wine bottle—a rich cabernet sauvignon.

"It's perfect," I assured him, taking the bottle. "I'll open it to breathe. Make yourself comfortable."

Chapter Four

♥

PENELOPE

Moving around the kitchen, I was acutely aware of Milo taking in my space. His gaze traveled over the colorful abstract paintings on the walls (picked up at various flea markets), the overflowing bookshelf in the corner (primarily cookbooks and romance novels), and finally settled on the collection of mismatched mugs hanging from hooks under the cabinets. Each item was a piece of me, a glimpse into who I was beyond the cheerful baker.

"Your place is... very you," he finally said, leaning against the kitchen counter.

I glanced over my shoulder as I uncorked the wine. "Is that a compliment or an observation that I live in cheerful chaos?"

The corner of his mouth twitched. "Can it be both?"

I laughed, pouring two glasses of wine. "I'll take it, then." I handed him a glass, trying to ignore the spark when our fingers brushed. "How's Rusty doing?"

Milo accepted the wine, taking a small sip before answering. "Better. His leg is healing well." He paused, studying me over the rim of his glass. "Wildlife Services picked him up this afternoon."

I sighed dramatically, turning to check on the chicken. "You're no fun at all, you know that? He liked us."

"He's a wild animal," Milo reminded me gently. "He doesn't 'like' anyone."

I shot him a knowing look over my shoulder. "He liked you. I can tell."

Milo's expression softened slightly, a reluctant smile tugging at his lips. "You think every creature likes me."

"Because they do," I replied, pulling the roasting pan from the oven. The chicken emerged golden and fragrant, surrounded by carrots, potatoes, and Brussels sprouts. "Animals know good people when they see them, even when those people try really hard to be grumpy and unapproachable."

"He's a wild animal, Penelope." Milo repeated.

"Who you probably talked to when no one was around," I teased, turning to plate the chicken. "I bet you told him all your deepest, darkest secrets."

When I glanced back, something in Milo's expression made my heart skip—a flicker of vulnerability quickly masked by his usual reserve. For a moment, I wondered if I'd hit closer to home than I'd intended.

"Sorry," I said softly. "I didn't mean to—"

"It's fine," he cut me off, his tone light but controlled. "For the record, the fox and I had a strictly professional relationship."

I laughed, relief washing over me as the moment of tension passed. "Well, I hope you at least told him goodbye from me."

"I did not," Milo said flatly, but a warmth in his eyes belied his tone. "Because that would be ridiculous."

"You absolutely did," I countered, grinning as I set the plates on my tiny dining table by the window. "Admit it."

Milo's lips twitched again, that almost smile I'd come to treasure. "The food looks amazing," he said, smoothly changing the subject.

I let him have the deflection, gesturing for him to sit. "I hope you like it. I don't cook for other people very often."

"You feed half the town daily," he pointed out, settling into the chair across from me.

"Baking's different," I said. "It's... I don't know. More forgiving. Cooking feels more complicated somehow."

Milo raised an eyebrow. "Forgiving? Sounds like you're just better at following the rules when sugar is involved."

I pressed a hand to my chest, mock offended. "I'll have you know I'm very precise when it comes to baking. It's everything else in life that's a bit... improvised."

"A bit?" Milo's eyes crinkled at the corners, and I found myself staring at how his entire face transformed when he smiled—really smiled, not just the fleeting half-smiles he usually offered.

"Fine," I conceded, lifting my wine glass. "A lot improvised. But that's what makes life interesting, don't you think? Following where the wind takes you, being open to unexpected adventures."

Milo's expression shifted slightly as he cut into his chicken. "Sometimes the wind leads you places you never wanted to go."

Something in his voice—a shadow, a weight—made me pause. This was the closest he'd ever come to referencing his past, the years before he'd settled in Anchor Bay. I knew from town gossip that he'd served as a veterinarian in the military, but he never spoke about it.

"And sometimes," I said gently, "it leads you exactly where you need to be, even if it's not where you planned."

His eyes met mine across the table, something unreadable flickering in their depths. "Is that what happened with you? The wind brought you to Anchor Bay?"

I smiled, grateful for the opening. "Sort of. I was actually on my way to Portland for a job interview at a fancy patisserie. I took a wrong turn, got a flat tire just outside town, and ended up at Maggie's Diner while I waited for the mechanic. I fell in love with the harbor view, and when I saw the 'For Sale' sign on the old Willoughby place..." I shrugged, remembering the moment of clarity I'd felt. "Something just clicked. Like I'd found a piece of myself I didn't know was missing."

Milo studied me, his expression thoughtful. "You gave up a job in Portland for a rundown bakery in a town you'd never heard of?"

"Best impulsive decision I ever made," I said without hesitation. "Though my parents thought I'd lost my mind. They still do, probably."

"They're not supportive?" Milo asked, his tone carefully neutral.

I traced the rim of my wine glass, considering how to answer. The topic of my parents always made me reflect in a way few things did.

"It's not that they're unsupportive," I said finally, looking up to meet Milo's attentive gaze. "They love me.

They've always made that clear. But they've never really... understood me."

I took a small sip of wine, gathering my thoughts. The rich cabernet warmed me, giving me courage to share parts of myself I rarely discussed.

"My parents are a lot like you, actually," I continued with a soft laugh. "Structured. Practical. Always thinking three steps ahead. My father's an accountant who color-codes his tie collection and has eaten the same breakfast every day for thirty years. My mother's a high school principal who plans her wardrobe for the entire month in advance."

Milo's eyebrows rose slightly. "And then there's you."

"And then there's me," I agreed, gesturing to myself with a self-deprecating smile. "The walking hurricane who can't keep plants alive but somehow remembers the precise ratio of flour to butter for seven different types of pastry. I was the kid who brought home stray animals, started a different hobby every week, and changed my college major three times before settling on culinary arts."

I paused, noticing Milo listening intently as if cataloging every detail. It made me feel simultaneously exposed and understood, sending warmth to my chest.

"They wanted me to follow my sister into something stable—law, medicine, or finance. Something with a clear path." I shrugged. "But I've never been good at following paths. I prefer making my own."

MILO

I watched as Penelope spoke about her family, fascinated by this glimpse into what had shaped her. It was easy to imagine her as a child—wild curls, perpetually scraped knees, pockets full of treasures she'd collected. Always in motion, always curious. The complete opposite of the disciplined, orderly childhood I'd had.

"Your sister followed the expected path?" I asked, curious about this other Everett who had apparently taken the road Penelope had abandoned.

Penelope nodded, her expression softening with obvious affection. "Piper. She's a corporate attorney in Seattle. She is brilliant and organized and has her whole life mapped out in a color-coded planner." She smiled into her wine glass. "We're complete opposites, but we're close. She pretends to be exasperated by my chaos but is my biggest supporter."

I couldn't help but smile at that. "She sounds like someone I'd get along with."

"Oh God," Penelope laughed, her eyes crinkling at the corners. "You two would be terrifying together. All that combined practicality in one room? The universe might implode."

The chicken was perfectly cooked, juicy, and fragrant with rosemary. I couldn't remember the last time I'd had a home-cooked meal like this—probably not since before Afghanistan. Most nights, I ate whatever was quickest after a long day at the clinic.

"This is really good," I said, gesturing to the food. "You've been holding out on me with just those scones."

Her smile brightened. "I knew it! You do like my scones!"

I rolled my eyes but couldn't suppress my answering smile. "Fine. Your cinnamon scones are the best thing I've tasted in Anchor Bay. Don't let it go to your head."

"Too late," she replied with a grin, topping off my wine glass. "I'm already planning to update my sign: 'Sweet Somethings: Home of Milo Turner's Favorite Scones'."

"You wouldn't dare," I said, though we both knew she absolutely would.

"What about you?" Penelope asked, her voice softer now. "How did you end up in Anchor Bay? The wind blow you here too?"

I hesitated, setting down my fork. This was dangerous territory. I'd spent three years carefully avoiding these conversations, deflecting questions about my past with practiced ease. But something about Penelope's open expression, the genuine interest in her eyes, made me want to offer at least a partial truth.

"Something like that," I said finally. "After my last tour in Afghanistan, I knew I was done. I needed space. Quiet." I took a sip of wine. "Opening a vet clinic seemed like a good place to start."

Penelope watched me carefully, and I could see her weighing whether to press further. I braced myself for the usual questions about combat, what I'd seen, and why I'd left. I deflected those questions so often, my answers were worn smooth, like river stones shaped by years of current.

Instead, she surprised me.

"Well, I'm glad the wind brought you here," she said simply, raising her glass in a small toast. "Whatever the reason."

The tightness in my chest eased slightly. This was what made Penelope different—she pushed, in some ways relentlessly, but somehow knew exactly when to step back.

"Even though I refuse to keep every stray animal you bring me?" I asked, grateful for the chance to lighten the mood.

Penelope laughed, the sound warming something in me that had been cold for a long time. "Especially because of that. Your grumpiness is part of your charm, you know."

"I'm not grumpy," I protested automatically. "I'm... reserved."

"Mmm-hmm," she hummed, clearly unconvinced. "Is that what we're calling it?"

"Well, you could call it professional or focused," I suggested, though my lips twitched.

"Grumpy," Penelope countered again, her eyes sparkling. "Brooding. Secretly soft-hearted but trying desperately to hide it."

I shook my head, unable to maintain my stern expression in the face of her teasing. "You're impossible."

"So I've been told," she replied, rising to clear our plates. "Often by you, actually."

I stood to help, gathering the silverware and following her to the small kitchen. A strand of fairy lights hung along the windowsill, reflecting in the darkened glass that looked out over Main Street. Outside, Anchor Bay was settling into evening – storefronts closing, streetlights flickering on one by one like stars appearing in the night sky.

As we worked side by side in the small space, I couldn't help but notice how naturally Penelope moved, her actions fluid and graceful despite the confined area. She hummed softly as she rinsed plates, a melody I didn't recognize but found oddly soothing. Her presence filled the kitchen – filled every room she occupied – with an energy that was both chaotic and comforting.

"You don't have to help," she said, glancing over her shoulder as I stacked plates in her dishwasher.

"I don't mind," I replied, oddly content in this domestic scene. "Seems only fair since you cooked."

"We need music," she declared, pulling out a small portable speaker. "Cleanup requires a soundtrack."

I watched as she connected her phone, scrolling through playlists with her thumb, her brow furrowed in concentration.

"Aha!" she exclaimed, selecting something with a triumphant tap. The opening notes of an old jazz standard filled the kitchen—Ella Fitzgerald, I realized with surprise.

I raised an eyebrow. "Ella Fitzgerald?"

Penelope grinned, swaying slightly to the music as she returned to the sink. "Don't look so shocked. I contain multitudes, Dr. Turner."

"Apparently," I murmured, handing her a glass to rinse.

She began to sing along softly, her voice warm and a little husky. It wasn't perfect, but it was genuine in a way that made my chest tighten. I found myself mesmerized by her.

Chapter Five

♥

PENELOPE

"Dance with me," I said suddenly, holding out my hand as Ella's velvet voice swelled around us, rich and timeless.

Milo froze, dish towel suspended in his hands like he'd been caught in the act of something scandalous. "What?"

I wiggled my fingers, still holding my hand out. "Dance with me."

"I don't dance, Penelope."

I huffed, stepping closer. "Everyone dances. Some people just need a little more convincing than others."

"Penelope," he warned, setting the towel down carefully. "I'm too old for this kind of thing."

I rolled my eyes. "You're not too *old*, you're too *stub-born*."

His expression remained unreadable, but I could see the battle behind those sharp, wary eyes. I knew what dancing meant. Closeness. Touch. It wasn't just about moving to the music; it was about acknowledging *this thing* between us that we both kept pretending didn't exist.

I softened my voice. "Come on, Milo. It's just a dance."

But we both knew it wasn't. Not really.

For a long moment, he hesitated, his lips pressed into a tight line as if deciding whether giving in was worth whatever storm was brewing inside him. Then, finally—*finally*—he reached for my hand.

His fingers were warm and rough, calloused in a way that told a thousand stories. My heart did something stupid in my chest when his grip tightened slightly.

I beamed up at him. "See? That wasn't so hard, was it?"

I placed his other hand on my waist, stepping close enough that the scent of his cologne wrapped around me. He didn't pull away, but his entire body was rigid, his movements stiff as I gently swayed to the music.

"Relax," I teased, watching him. "You look like someone's holding you at gunpoint."

"I feel like an idiot," he muttered as we narrowly avoided bumping into my refrigerator. "This kitchen is too small for dancing."

I laughed, swaying us in another tiny circle. "No, it's perfect. You just need to loosen up."

He exhaled sharply, but something in his shoulders eased—just a fraction, but I noticed. His hand at my waist tightened, and I felt it *everywhere.*

For a few moments, we just moved, the fairy lights above the sink casting silver flecks in his eyes. I was painfully aware of every point of contact between us—his palm against mine, his hand at my waist, the way our bodies fit together despite our height difference.

It wasn't just dancing anymore.

It was *something else.*

I felt his breath hitch. My own chest rose and fell in time with his.

"Milo," I whispered, my voice barely audible over the music.

Something flickered in his gaze—something raw and unsure and entirely too honest.

The music swelled around us, Ella's voice dipping and soaring like a bird in flight. Milo's eyes never left mine, blue and deep as the harbor at twilight. I could feel the tension in his body—not resistance anymore, but something else entirely. Something electric and inevitable.

"Penelope," he murmured, my name a question and answer all at once.

Time seemed to slow, stretching between us. The kitchen disappeared—the fairy lights, the dishes in the sink, the remnants of dinner—until there was nothing but this moment, suspended.

His hand at my waist slid to the small of my back, drawing me closer until I could feel the steady rhythm of his heartbeat against my chest. Not so steady now, I realized with a flutter of triumph. It raced beneath his ribs, matching the wild cadence of my own.

I watched the conflict play across his face—desire warring with restraint, want battling caution. In the soft glow of the fairy lights, I could see each emotion as it flickered through his eyes: longing, uncertainty, and, beneath it all, a vulnerability that made my heart ache. This close, I noticed details I'd never seen—a small scar above his left eyebrow, how thick his eyelashes were, and a tiny freckle near his temple.

"Penelope," he said again, my name rough.

I don't know which of us moved first. Maybe we both did, pulled by the same invisible thread tugging us together since that first day in his clinic. One moment, we were swaying in my tiny kitchen, barely moving to Ella's crooning, and the next, his lips were on mine, warm and sure and *right*.

I pressed closer, rising on my tiptoes, one hand sliding up to curl around the nape of his neck.

That was all the encouragement he needed. His arms tightened around me, lifting me slightly as his mouth moved against mine with newfound urgency. The tentative kiss transformed into something more profound, hungrier. My fingers threaded through his hair, anchoring him to me as if he might disappear if I let go.

He tasted like the wine we'd shared, rich and intoxicating, and I found myself dizzy with wanting more.

MILO

She kissed me like I was something good.

Like I wasn't made of scars and silence. Like I hadn't just spent the last decade convincing myself that I didn't deserve this.

And I kissed her back.

God, I kissed her back like I'd been starving for it.

Because I had been.

Her fingers curled at the back of my neck, her mouth warm and sure, and for a second—just one breathtaking, impossible second—I let myself believe I could stay.

But then I felt it.

The shift.

Not in her—but in me.

That familiar pull of panic, rising fast. The instinct to retreat before I ruined it. Before I let her see the parts of me that weren't steady hands and clever banter. The parts that woke me in the middle of the night, chest heaving, heart racing with memories that didn't fade.

She deserved someone who could give her more than that. More than *me*.

I pulled back, slowly at first—but then all at once.

The air between us cooled as I stepped away, her hand slipping from mine like a lifeline I was too scared to grab.

Her lips were still parted when I pulled away.

Still warm. Still tasting like hope.

"I have to go," I said, my voice rough and uneven. "Early morning tomorrow."

It was a terrible excuse. A coward's out.

But it was all I could manage with my heart pounding and her taste still on my lips.

Her expression crumpled, just slightly—but enough.

Enough to gut me.

She blinked like she couldn't quite process what was happening. She was still standing in that moment, her heart wide open while I was already walking away.

"Milo," she said softly, her voice cracking on my name. "What just happened?"

I looked at her—and immediately regretted it.

She looked lost. Confused. Hurt.

Like she'd finally handed someone the fragile thing she'd been protecting and was watching it get dropped without warning.

I forced myself to look away, grabbed my jacket, and blurted out the most useless thing imaginable. "Dinner was great. Thank you."

Her arms crossed over her chest like she was trying to hold herself together. "Is that it?"

Her voice wasn't angry. It wasn't cold.

It was worse.

It was quiet.

"I'll let you know how Rusty does with Wildlife Services," I muttered halfway to the door. Already unraveling.

She didn't respond this time. Didn't nod. Didn't smile.

Just stood there in her kitchen, fairy lights glowing above her.

I opened the door and stepped into the night.

I could feel her watching me go.

***

I drove home too fast, my knuckles white against the steering wheel. The dark coastal road stretched ahead, moonlight glinting off the water to my left as I wound my way back to my cabin on the edge of town. My house sat alone on a bluff overlooking the ocean, isolated by design. I'd chosen it precisely because it kept me apart from the rest of Anchor Bay—a buffer between me and a world I wasn't sure I belonged in anymore.

I pulled into my gravel driveway, killed the engine, and just... sat there. The quiet pressed in from all sides as I let my head fall against the seat, trying to understand what I'd just done.

I'd kissed her.

I'd kissed Penelope Everett in her kitchen, wrapped in fairy lights, cinnamon, and laughter.

And then I'd left her standing there—confused, hurt, reaching for something I couldn't give her.

God.

I could still feel her in my arms, the subtle weight of her hand in mine, the way she looked at me. The music, the low golden light, her warmth pressed against me—it had all felt like a dream I had no right to step into.

I finally forced myself out of the truck. The cold night air hit me like a reprimand. I crossed the front porch, unlocked the door, and entered my dark, silent house.

Everything about it felt wrong.

Sterile furniture. Bare walls. No music. No color. The kind of place you stayed in, but didn't really live in.

I went through the motions.

Filled a glass of water I didn't drink.

Checked the locks. Flipped light switches that didn't need flipping—just to keep my hands busy.

Brushed my teeth like routine could scrub out the ache.

But it couldn't.

Because my mind kept circling back to her.

To the kiss. To the softness of her sweater under my hands. To the way she looked up at me like I was worth waiting for—even when I kept proving I wasn't.

What was I doing?

Getting involved with Penelope would be a mistake—for both of us. She deserved someone whole. Someone who didn't still wake up at 3 am expecting mortar fire and the taste of sand in his mouth. Someone who hadn't already lived three lives and felt worn out by all of them.

Someone who didn't carry a decade's worth of ghosts tucked under his ribs.

I made my way to bed, but sleep didn't come easy. I lay there, staring at the ceiling, the crash of waves against the cliffs below normally a comfort—but not tonight.

Tonight, all I could hear was her laughter. All I could feel was the way she fit against me. The way she'd whispered my name like a promise.

Whatever this was—this pull toward her that defied all logic, that cracked open places I thought I'd permanently sealed shut—it needed to end before I hurt her. Because that's what would happen.

People like me didn't get second chances at something real. Not after everything I'd seen. Not after everything I'd failed to save.

Not after everything I'd already lost.

I turned toward the window, eyes open in the dark, listening to the sound of the sea and trying to convince myself I'd done the right thing.

But the ache in my chest wouldn't let me believe it.

Not really.

Chapter Six

♥

PENELOPE

The morning light filtered through my kitchen window, casting a golden glow across the room where Milo and I had danced just hours before. I cradled my coffee mug between both hands, letting the warmth seep into my fingers as I replayed last night's events for what felt like the hundredth time.

My dreams had been filled with Milo—his hands on my waist, his eyes darkening as we swayed in my kitchen, and then... more. Much more than had actually happened.

I sighed, running a hand through my unruly morning curls. Something had shifted between us in that kiss. I'd felt it—the way his breath hitched, the way his hands trembled just slightly as they held mine. For a brief, perfect moment, I'd believed he wanted this too. Wanted me.

But then he'd pulled away, retreating behind his carefully constructed walls.

This was ridiculous. I was a grown woman pining after a man who had literally run away rather than spend another minute with me. If that wasn't a clear signal, I didn't know what was.

"Get it together, Penelope," I muttered.

The bakery wouldn't open itself, and I had wedding favors to finish for the Hendersons.

I drained my coffee, rinsed the mug in the sink, and headed downstairs to the bakery. The space was still and quiet in the early morning hours—my favorite time, before the bustle of customers and the day's chaos began. The scent of yesterday's baking lingered faintly in the air—cinnamon, vanilla, and the yeasty promise of bread. I flipped on the lights, watching my little kingdom come to life.

Sweet Somethings wasn't fancy like the upscale patisseries I'd trained in. The walls were warm, butter yellow, and the floors were worn hardwood that creaked in certain spots. Mismatched vintage tables and chairs were arranged throughout the front, each one a treasure I'd found at various flea markets and antique shops along the coast.

The display cases—my pride and joy—gleamed beneath the pendant lights, waiting to be filled with the day's offerings. This space had become more than just a business to me; it was an extension of myself, a physical manifestation of the dreams I'd carried since I was eight years old, standing on a step stool in my grandmother's kitchen, learning to fold pastry dough.

I tied my apron around my waist and got to work, losing myself in the familiar rhythm of baking. There was comfort in the precision of measurements, the feel of dough beneath my fingers, and the transformation of simple ingredients into something magical. By the time my assistant, Lucy, arrived at six, I'd already produced three trays of scones, two dozen muffins, and was elbow-deep in wedding favor preparation.

"Morning, boss," Lucy called, hanging her jacket on the hook by the back door. She was a college student with bright eyes, a bright mind, and no fear of my early-morning mood.

"You're early," I said without looking up. "Is everything okay?"

She shrugged. "Yep, just couldn't sleep. Figured I'd come in and wrestle with the espresso machine."

"That machine likes you better than me," I muttered. "Last week, it tried to steam my fingerprints off."

She grinned and headed toward the front to prep the coffee bar. I turned my attention back to the favors, trying not to let my thoughts wander *again* to a certain gruff, broody vet who spun me around my kitchen like I was something fragile. And then left like I was something dangerous.

The bell over the front door jingled just as I finished the wedding favors.

Lucy popped her head into the kitchen. "Uh, Penelope? You've got a visitor."

My stomach fluttered. I already knew who it was.

I wiped my hands on a towel and stepped out front.

There he was. Milo Turner. All six feet-something of gruff, frustrating, emotionally unavailable man, standing in the middle of my bakery like he didn't have the emotional range of a rock. He looked... tired. But not in an overworked way. More like *I didn't sleep because I was thinking about something I didn't want to think about*, kind of tired.

He glanced around the shop. "Can we...?" He motioned toward one of the empty tables.

I hesitated, then nodded, walking over and sitting down.

We sat in silence for a beat too long.

"I owe you an apology," Milo said, the words landing heavier than I expected.

I froze. He wasn't a man who apologized readily.

He sat across from me, elbows on the table, shoulders tense. "Last night... I shouldn't have left like that. I just—" He exhaled, rough and shaky. "You deserve better than me, Penelope."

I blinked. "Excuse me?"

"You deserve someone who isn't—" He scrubbed a hand over his face, frustration tightening his jaw. "Who isn't old, jaded, and haunted by things you'll never understand. Someone who can keep up with your energy, your optimism... your heart."

My chest tightened. "Is that supposed to be some noble sacrifice, Milo?"

He flinched but didn't stop. "I've seen what happens when people count on me. I've seen what it looks like to try and save something, only to watch it slip through your fingers. I've held dying animals in my arms. I've held dying soldiers." His voice cracked on the last word, and for a heartbeat, he didn't speak.

"You live in color, Penelope," he said finally. "You see beauty everywhere. You reach for things—people, animals, hope—and try to fix what's broken. But I've lived in the dark too long. I don't know how to let go of it. I don't know how to be what you need."

Anger flared hot and sharp in my chest. "So what, you decided to preemptively walk away before I figure that out for myself?"

His gaze snapped to mine. "No. I'm trying to keep you from making a mistake."

"No," I shot back, rising from the table, my voice climbing. "You're trying to justify running. You're trying to make it sound like protection, but really, you're afraid. Of me. Of this. Because it's messy and real."

Milo stood, slower, every movement controlled—like he was holding himself together by sheer will. "This is messy. You bring chaos with you, Penelope. You feel everything... too much. You care too deeply. And I've spent years trying to survive the kind of chaos that destroys people."

His words hit like a slap. "So I'm a liability now?"

"I didn't say that," he said quietly.

"You didn't have to," I whispered, my throat tight.

He looked away, jaw clenched. "You should be with someone who doesn't look at joy and wonder when it'll be taken away. Someone who doesn't flinch when things get too good. Someone who won't crush it just because he doesn't believe it'll last."

"That's not about what I need, Milo. That's about what *you're afraid of*." I said, the words catching in my throat. "You're afraid of someone who makes you feel too deeply."

His silence was answer enough.

And just like that, the bottom fell out of my chest.

I stepped back, breath shaking. "You're doing exactly what he did, Milo. You're making me feel like I'm too much. Too loud. Too hopeful. Too me."

His eyes flew to mine, pain written across every line of his face—but he didn't say a word.

Didn't reach for me.

Didn't fight.

And that hurt more than anything he could have said.

"Go," I whispered, voice breaking. "Before I say something I'll regret."

The silence between us cracked wide open. He nodded once—barely—and turned toward the door.

As it closed behind him, the bakery felt colder. Emptier.

MILO

The bell over the bakery door jingled as I stepped out, but the sound felt like it came from another world. The one I didn't belong in.

I walked blindly past the flower shop, the bookstore, and a family of tourists taking selfies near the boardwalk arch. My boots hit the pavement with dull, measured thuds, each echoing louder in my head than it should.

I hadn't just messed up. I'd ruined *everything*.

She'd been standing there, apron streaked with powdered sugar and heartbreak, looking at me like I was the one thing in her life that had finally broken her in a way she hadn't expected. And maybe I had. Hell, I probably had.

Because I couldn't handle the brightness. The hope. The way she made the world feel *possible* again.

I didn't belong in her life. I belonged in sterile exam rooms and surgical routines. In silence. In control. I'd spent years building that. Rebuilding it, really—after the noise and chaos of war had hollowed me out.

And then she came along.

All warm colors and wild curls. Laughing in my clinic, tracking flour across my floors like she owned every inch of the world she touched. She made my life feel too *full*, too *unpredictable*. She made me want things I didn't believe I could have anymore.

She made me want *her*.

And it terrified the hell out of me.

I stopped walking when I reached the edge of the beach, the salty wind slapping against my face like it was trying to knock some damn sense into me. I stared at the ocean, hands shoved deep into my pockets.

I hadn't meant to hurt her.

But I had.

And now? It was too late. I'd seen how she crumbled when she turned away, even if she didn't want me to.

She wasn't going to forgive me.

She *shouldn't* forgive me.

She was sunlight.

And I'd spent so long in the dark

Chapter Seven

♥

PENELOPE

I sat at the little table in my apartment above the bakery, a half-drunk chamomile tea going cold beside me and the weight of too many unsaid things pressing against my chest.

I didn't plan to write him a letter. Honestly, I thought I was done crying over Milo Turner. But the words wouldn't stop spinning through my head, and I needed them out.

So I grabbed the nearest pen and the back of a bakery order form and started to write.

Dear Milo,

You'll probably never read this. I'm not writing it for you—not really. I'm writing it for me. Because if I don't let these words out, they'll sit in my chest like stones, and I'm tired of carrying things that don't belong to me. I wanted you to be different. I hoped you would be. And maybe that's what stings the most. Because I let myself believe—for one fragile second—that you saw me. Not just the woman who takes in broken things and sees beauty in the wreckage... but the woman underneath it all. People have always told me I'm too much. Too loud. Too sensitive. Too... everything. My ex-husband said I lived in a dream world like that was a flaw. He told me I cared too much about things that didn't matter. That I expected too much from people. That I was foolish. And for a long time, I believed him. I shrank myself to fit into the narrow space he made for me. I tried to be less. Less loud. Less sensitive. Less me. But deep down, I never stopped wanting to be loved as I am. For who I am. And then you came along. Grumpy, quiet, and closed off—but kind in the ways that mattered. You didn't run when I showed up with a fox tucked in my coat. You didn't scoff when I freaked out over a goat demolishing my pastries. You danced with me in my kitchen. You held me like I was something precious. And for a little while, I thought maybe I wasn't too much for you. But then you left. And that hurt more than I expected. But what hurt even more was what you said when you came back. The way you looked at me like I was a storm you barely survived. The way you said I was chaos—that I was something dangerous you couldn't afford to get involved with. That moment felt like confirmation. That the people I care for will always decide I'm too much. Too complicated. Too hopeful. Too me. But here's the thing I realized after you walked away, Milo:

I'm not too much. I am me. And I won't apologize for it anymore. I'm the kind of woman who builds things from scratch—recipes, routines, entire lives—sprinkled with sugar and stitched together with heart. I cry over hurt an-

imals, name the squirrels outside my window, laugh too loud in quiet rooms, and love like I don't know how to stop. I try, even when it hurts. Especially then. I'm not sorry for that. Not anymore. I'm not writing this to make you feel bad or to ask for anything in return. I'm writing this to let go— Of the hope that you would be different. Of the weight I carried, thinking it was my fault you weren't. I could have loved you, Milo. But I chose to love myself instead. And the next time someone asks you to dance in a kitchen, I hope you say yes. For her. For you. Goodbye.

Penelope

I stared at the letter for a long time, my thumb smudging a bit of ink near the bottom.

Then I folded it in half and tucked it into my apron pocket because I couldn't quite bring myself to throw it away.

***

I stepped outside to put the day's menu out, and that's when I saw it.

A flicker of movement near the flower box.

I squinted, thinking it was a leaf caught in the breeze, but then it shifted again, trembling. I knelt down, heart already climbing into my throat.

A baby rabbit.

Tiny. Shivering. One paw curled beneath it at a strange angle.

"Oh no," I breathed, easing my apron off and gently scooping the little thing into it. "You poor, sweet baby."

It didn't fight. Just burrowed into the soft fabric like it had been waiting for someone to notice it was hurting.

I stood there, holding it close, unsure of what to do. Milo would know.

But I didn't call him.

I couldn't.

Not after everything that had been said—and everything that hadn't.

So I called the wildlife rescue group in Granite Falls instead. They were familiar, and they didn't ask questions. Just told me to bring the bunny over as soon as I could.

I added a towel to a small box for warmth, then gently placed the bunny—still bundled in my apron—inside.

It didn't struggle. Just curled into the softness like it finally had permission to rest.

I grabbed my keys, locked the bakery, and headed to Granite Falls.

The drive was quiet except for the soft rustle from the passenger seat. I glanced over and offered a gentle smile.

"It's okay, sweetheart. You're gonna be alright," I murmured. "They'll take good care of you. Better than I could."

The bunny didn't move, but I kept talking anyway. About the weather, the cookies I'd burnt yesterday morning, and the names I could've given it if this were any other day.

By the time I pulled up to the wildlife center, my heart had settled just a little.

I carried the box inside, handed it to a kind-looking volunteer, and gave a quick, quiet thank you.

MILO

I was only in Granite Falls for the day, filling in for their regular vet, who was at a conference. It wasn't unusual—they called me whenever they were short, and I didn't mind the change of pace.

Most days, it was injured squirrels or birds tangled in fishing lines. Quiet work. Simple, in the best way.

Then I opened the box with the baby rabbit.

Tiny. Shaking. One paw curled at a bad angle. I moved the towel to get a better look and froze.

It wasn't a towel.

It was an apron.

Light blue, soft from too many washes, and stitched across the front in delicate thread: *Sweet Somethings.*

Penelope's bakery.

My chest went tight.

I stared at it briefly, like it might suddenly be from somewhere else. Someone else. But I'd know that apron anywhere.

I stepped out to the front desk. "Hey—who brought in the rabbit?"

The volunteer glanced at the clipboard. "No name. The woman dropped it off maybe twenty minutes ago. Said she didn't want a callback. Just asked us to take care of it."

She hadn't called me. She'd driven to the next town over just to avoid me. It wasn't about the rabbit. It was about drawing a line—one I'd forced her to draw. Because I'd made it clear I couldn't be trusted with anything fragile. Not even her hope.

I went back into the exam room and ran my fingers along the edge of the box, like maybe I could still catch some trace of her warmth. The rabbit stirred, and I reached to settle the apron more securely around him. That's when I heard it—the quiet crinkle of something hidden in the folds.

I reached into the pocket and pulled out a folded sheet of paper.

My name was written at the top.

Dear Milo...

I didn't think. I just read.

By the end, I wasn't breathing.

It wasn't just the words that wrecked me.

It was the truth inside them.

Not just the part where I hurt her—that would've been enough.

But the part where she got back up.

The part where she chose to love herself when I didn't.

Where she said she wouldn't shrink, wouldn't apologize, wouldn't wait for someone to catch up.

Because I remembered how small her voice had gone when I said what I said. I remembered the look on her face when I told her she felt too big, too intense like she was pressing into all the corners of a life I'd tried to keep neatly contained.

But she *wasn't* too much.

She never had been.

She was joy and heart and warmth. She made things better just by being in the room. She gave everything—*everything*—without asking for anything in return except to be seen.

And I made her question that.

That's what wrecked me.

I stared at the letter, the words still ringing like a bell.

She hadn't written it to make me feel bad.

She hadn't written it for *me* at all.

But I felt every word like it was carved straight into my chest.

Not because she was broken.

Because I finally saw how whole she really was.

She'd always been that fierce. That full of heart. That steady, even in her wildness. I just hadn't been strong enough to stand beside it. I tried to shrink it. Control it. Make it quieter because I couldn't handle what it made me feel about *myself*.

I folded the letter with slow, careful hands and looked down at the rabbit, still nestled in her apron. Of course she'd wrapped him in something soft. Of course she'd made space for something small and scared. That's who she was.

She saved everything she touched. Not with grand gestures or loud declarations—But with steady, quiet grace.

She hadn't written the letter for me. She hadn't asked for anything. She hadn't left a door open.

But for the first time, I let myself hope—Not that she was waiting. Not that she'd take me back.

But that maybe... just maybe... I could become the man she once believed I was. And maybe, buried somewhere beneath the wreckage, there was still something in me worth saving.

***

The bakery was still dark, the sign flipped to *Closed*, morning dew clinging to the windows.

I stood outside holding her apron, folded and clean, the same one she'd wrapped around the injured bunny like it was something sacred. Inside the front pocket, I left a note.

Not to match hers—nothing could—but to answer it. Quietly. Honestly. Without expectation.

I set it gently on the top step, reached up, and rang the bell.

Just once.

Then I turned and walked away.

Chapter Eight

♥

PENELOPE

The bell rang just once. A single, polite chime that pulled me away from the kettle hissing upstairs.

I padded barefoot down the stairs, tugging my sweater tight around me, expecting a delivery dropped off too early or maybe a neighbor with a question about weekend pastries.

But when I opened the door, no one was there. Just a pale blue shape sitting neatly on the top step. My apron.

I stared at it, blinking against the morning light like I might be confused. It was clean. Folded. Familiar in a way that made something shift in my chest.

How did one of my aprons end up out here?

I bent down, fingertips brushing the soft fabric. And then it clicked. The bunny. This must've been the one I wrapped it in.

I hadn't even thought about what I'd used until now. I was so focused on keeping it warm, on getting it to Granite Falls safely... I must have just handed the whole thing over. It was sweet, whoever had taken the time to return it.

I exhaled slowly, thumb brushing the corner of the pocket.

Then I felt it—something inside the pocket.

A slip of paper.

I frowned, heart ticking up a little. My first thought was *the* letter. The one I wrote and never meant to give to anyone. The one I'd tucked into that exact pocket before I found the rabbit.

"Oh no," I whispered, reaching in.

But when I pulled it out, my breath caught.

Different paper. Different ink.

Not mine.

I unfolded it slowly, pulse now humming in my ears.

Penelope,

I know you didn't mean for me to see your letter. I was filling in at the clinic when you dropped off the bunny. I didn't know it was you—not at first. Not until I saw the apron. When I examined the rabbit, I shifted the fabric and felt something in the pocket. That's when I found your letter. I knew it was personal. I knew it wasn't meant for me. But my name was at the top, and before I could stop myself...I read it.

My throat tightened. My fingers gripped the fabric of the apron like it might hold me steady.

He *read* it.

And this—this was *his* letter.

I looked down at the rest of the page, heart raw and wide open.

Then I kept reading.

And it broke me. Not because you were angry. You weren't. You were honest. Brave. Everything I wasn't. You were never too much. I was just too afraid of what it meant to care that deeply. I let my damage speak louder than my heart. And instead of facing that, I made it your problem. You offered me light—And I dimmed it, just to make my shadows feel comfortable. Reading your letter didn't just show me what I lost. It showed me what I'd failed to see: That your hope, your fire, your wild, soft heart...It wasn't chaos. It was courage. It's what made me want to be better. Still does. You said you chose to love yourself instead. And you were right to. This letter isn't a plea. It's not a fix-it or a grand gesture. It's just this: I see you now. And I'm sorry I didn't sooner. If there's even the smallest part of you that wonders whether there might still be something here—Something worth mending—I'll be here. Not to change you. Not to calm you. But to walk beside you. As you are.

—Milo

The letter sat on the counter for hours after I read it. Folded. Unfolded. Folded again.

I wasn't sure if it was an ending... or a beginning.

Part of me—the part who still believed people can surprise you in the best ways—wanted to believe he meant it.

That he saw me. Really saw me.

And maybe... that was worth the risk.

Not everything, not all at once.

But enough for one small gesture.

I decided to make scones. The cinnamon ones he couldn't resist.

I didn't overthink it.

I didn't write a note.

I packed them in a box, tied it with twine, and drove to his house.

MILO

I heard the knock. When I opened the door, she was standing there, holding a bakery box. Cinnamon hung in the air. Penelope.

Here.

For a second, neither of us moved. Then I stepped back. "Will you come in?"

She held my gaze—steady, thoughtful. Then she nodded. "Yeah," she said softly. "I'd like that."

She stepped past me, the box still in her hands, and something in the air shifted—like a pressure I hadn't realized I was holding loosened in my chest. I closed the door behind her.

For a moment, we just stood there. The silence wasn't awkward. It was full of hope, longing. She glanced around the room—not inspecting, just noticing.

I gestured to the box in her hands. "What's the occasion?"

She met my eyes. No hesitation. "Because maybe I'm not done hoping yet."

Something cracked open in my chest—quiet, but deep.

I didn't deserve that kind of grace. Not after what I put her through. But she was here. And I wasn't going to waste it.

I took the box from her and set it on the counter gently, like it might break. Turned back to her.

"I've been hoping," I said. "Even when I didn't think I had the right to. "She didn't say anything. But she didn't look away. "I meant every word," I added. "Of the note. Of all of it. "I just stood there—ready to show her, not beg her.

Then I did the only thing that felt honest.

I reached out my hand. "Dance with me. "A breath hung between us. Her eyebrows lifted—like the words caught her off guard, but in the best possible way. "In your living room?" she asked.

I nodded. "Wherever you are—that's where I want to be."

She stepped in. Slipped her hand into mine.

We didn't need music. We just moved—slow and easy—right there in my living room. Like there was nowhere else we needed to be.

We talked about everything and nothing. Laughed in soft moments. Fell quiet in others.

And when the hours stretched long and the night settled deep, she was still there—Still in my arms.

And for the first time in a long time, the darkness didn't take hold. Because she chose to stay. And share her light.

Epilogue

♥

MILO

Some mornings still came with shadows.

But now, when I woke up to find Penelope curled against me—warm, soft, tangled in the sheets and somehow always stealing my half of the blanket—I didn't flinch at the light.

I reached for it. For her. Every time.

She filled the kitchen with music and flour and bursts of laughter I still wasn't sure I deserved. And every time she danced across the floor in her apron, I just watched—grateful, amazed, still a little stunned that she stayed.

Not because I asked her to. But because she wanted to.

She was at the stove now, humming to some old song drifting through the speakers, her hair piled in a messy knot, flour dusted across one cheek.

I leaned against the doorway, watching her move, and that ache in my chest—less pain now, more wonder—settled into something deeper.

"You're staring," she said without turning around.

"I know," I said. "Can't help it."

She glanced over her shoulder, smirking. "If you're going to stare like that, you'd better come over here and make yourself useful."

I pushed off the frame and crossed the room. Slid my arms around her waist. Let myself feel the warmth of her, the soft give of her body against mine, the way she didn't pull away.

"I was thinking," I murmured, brushing my lips against her neck, "about how lucky I am that you came back."

Her hands covered mine on her hips. "I didn't just come back," she said quietly. "I stayed."

She turned in my arms, eyes searching mine.

I kissed her then. Slow. Certain. Like everything we'd been through had led to this moment—this choice to love each other, fully and without fear.

My hands traced the curve of her waist as I deepened the kiss, savoring the soft gasp that escaped her lips. She tasted like cinnamon and coffee, warm and familiar and still somehow thrilling after all this time.

"The pancakes are going to burn," she murmured against my mouth, though her fingers were already threading through my hair, contradicting her words.

"Let them," I whispered, trailing kisses along her jaw, down the column of her throat.

She laughed, the sound vibrating against my lips. "You're terrible."

"Only for you," I said, reaching behind her to turn off the stove.

Her eyes darkened as she watched me, something wild and wanting flashing across her face.

"Take me to bed, Milo," she said softly.

I lifted her, her legs wrapping around my waist as I carried her through the hallway. The house that had once felt too empty, too quiet, now held echoes of her laughter in every corner.

I carried Penelope to our bedroom, her weight familiar and perfect in my arms. Sunlight streamed through the half-drawn curtains, painting golden stripes across the rumpled sheets we'd left behind earlier. Her eyes held mine, warm hazel catching the light, showing flecks of amber and green I'd memorized over countless mornings like this one.

"You're thinking too much," she whispered, brushing her thumb across my furrowed brow as I laid her gently on the bed.

"Just appreciating the view," I said, voice rough with wanting her.

She smiled up at me—that smile that had first cracked my carefully constructed walls—and reached for the hem of her oversized t-shirt. My t-shirt, actually, stolen from my drawer months ago and claimed as her own. She lifted it slowly, revealing herself inch by inch until she tossed it aside with a flourish.

The sight of her took my breath away—not just her beauty, but the openness in her expression, the trust in her eyes. This gift of vulnerability she offered without hesitation.

"I love you," I said, the words coming easier now than they once had.

Penelope smiled, reaching for me. "I know. Now come here and show me."

I joined her on the bed, my weight dipping the mattress as I moved over her. Our lips met in a slow, deliberate kiss that quickly deepened into something hungrier. Her hands found the buttons of my shirt, working them open with practiced ease until she could push the fabric from my shoulders.

Her fingers traced the scars on my chest—reminders of a life before her—with a reverence that still humbled me.

Her palm rested against my chest, her touch warming the scar tissue beneath. The sensation traveled through me, igniting something primal yet tender. I captured her hand, bringing it to my lips to kiss each fingertip—the ones that created delicate pastries and caressed broken things back to wholeness. Including me.

Penelope reached between us, wrapping her fingers around my thick length. I groaned, my hips jerking involuntarily at her touch.

"I want you inside me," Penelope whispered, never shy to tell me what she wanted.

"God, yes," I breathed, kissing her lips quickly before stripping the rest of my clothing off.

My muscles tensed as I pushed into Penelope, her soft and yielding walls welcoming me with a velvet embrace. A rush of heat flooded my body, and I marveled at how perfect our union was. A primal moan escaped Penelope's lips as her hips instinctively moved to meet my thrust. Buried to the hilt, I held still for a moment.

"More," Penelope whispered, moving her hips. "Please, don't stop."

I chuckled, Penelope could be so demanding. "Not a chance," I said softly.

I withdrew slowly before sinking back into her warmth, establishing a steady rhythm that had us both breathing heavily. Her fingers dug into my shoulders, urging me closer, deeper. I obliged, losing myself in the sensation of her body beneath mine, around mine, completely entwined with mine.

"Yes," she gasped, arching to meet each thrust. "Just like that."

I watched her face as pleasure overtook her—the flutter of her eyelashes, the parting of her lips, the flush spreading across her chest. This was Penelope at her most honest, most vulnerable, most beautiful.

"Look at me," I whispered, needing to see her eyes when she came undone.

Her gaze locked with mine, hazel depths swimming with emotion and desire. I felt her begin to tighten around me, her breathing growing more erratic.

"Milo," she breathed, my name a prayer on her lips as her body trembled beneath mine. Her fingers clutched my shoulders, eyes holding mine as waves of pleasure washed over her. The sight of her coming undone pushed me toward my own release.

"I love you," I whispered against her neck as I followed her over the edge, my body shuddering with the force of my climax.

We lay tangled together afterward, her head on my chest, my fingers tracing lazy patterns on her bare shoulder. Sunlight streamed through the windows, warming our skin as our breathing slowly returned to normal.

"The pancakes are definitely ruined," she murmured, pressing a kiss to my chest.

I laughed, the sound rumbling beneath her ear. "Worth it."

She propped herself up on one elbow, studying my face with that gentle curiosity that always made me feel like I was a puzzle she was constantly solving—and delighting in each new discovery.

"What?" I asked, tucking a stray curl behind her ear.

"Just thinking about how far we've come," she said softly. "From that grumpy vet who scolded me for bringing in strays to... this."

I smiled, memories of those early days washing over me—her determined optimism colliding with my carefully constructed walls. "I wasn't that grumpy."

"You absolutely were," she laughed, poking my chest playfully. "You practically growled at me when I brought in that seagull."

"The one with the broken wing that somehow ended up with a name and a backstory within five minutes of you finding it?"

"Captain Feathers had been through a lot," she defended solemnly, though her eyes danced with mischief. "He deserved respect."

I traced my finger along her collarbone, smiling at the memory. "That bird tried to take a chunk out of my hand."

"He was expressing his individuality," she countered, leaning into my touch.

I laughed, pulling her closer. "You and your strays. Always seeing the best in everything."

Her expression softened as she met my eyes. "Including you."

The words hung between us, simple but profound. Because she had seen the best in me when I couldn't see it in myself. When all I could focus on were the broken pieces, the shadows, the parts I thought made me unworthy of someone like her.

"Especially me," I agreed quietly, pressing a kiss to her forehead.

She sighed, content, curling closer like she belonged there—which she did. I held her a little tighter, letting the quiet settle around us. We'd come a long way. And we still had more to learn, more to face, more to build. But we were doing it together. And for the first time in a long time, the future didn't feel like something to brace for. It felt like something to look forward to.

***

Dear Reader,

Thank you so much for reading *A Heart Worth Mending*! I hope you were swept up in Penelope and Milo's journey—the quiet tension, the slow-burning connection, and the way two beautifully imperfect people found their way to healing and hope. Writing their story was deeply special to me, and I'm so grateful you came along for every heartfelt, tender, and sometimes laugh-out-loud moment.

If you enjoyed the book, I'd be so thankful if you took a moment to leave a review. Reviews help authors like me reach more readers, and even a short note makes a big difference in sharing these stories with the world.

Thank you for your support—I can't wait to bring you more swoony, emotional, high-heat romances filled with heart, humor, and characters worth believing in.

With love,

Hana York

***

Loved *A Heart Worth Mending*? Don't miss the rest of the *Hearts on Duty* series! Each book is packed with swoon-worthy heroes, strong heroines, and plenty of sparks. If you haven't read them yet, here's what you're missing:

Book One

Sparks of Temptation

A sizzling small-town romance where forced proximity turns up the heat between a stubborn chef and

a protective firefighter. Olivia Harper came to Anchor Bay for a fresh start—not a flirty distraction. After rebuilding her life, she has no time for complications, especially the kind that come with broad shoulders, a cocky grin, and a hero complex. Jack Lawson knows how to keep his cool under pressure. As a firefighter, protecting people is second nature. But Olivia? She doesn't want rescuing, and she sure as hell doesn't want him getting too close. When a plumbing mishap lands him as her unexpected housemate, their battle of wills turns into something neither of them can ignore. The problem? Olivia has spent years proving she doesn't need anyone, while Jack's instincts tell him to stand back before he wants something he can't have. But some flames refuse to die out...

Book Two

Love's Anchor

A sizzling small-town romance where years of friendship ignite into something neither of them can ignore. Brooke Taylor has spent years keeping her feelings for Theo Morgan buried beneath sharp comebacks and stubborn denial. As a no-nonsense cop in Anchor Bay, she's never let emotions get in the way of the job—especially when it comes to the charming, frustrating bar owner who knows exactly how to push her buttons. Theo has always played it safe when it comes to Brooke. She's his best friend, his steady constant—the one woman he can't afford to lose. But when a break-in at his bar forces them into close quarters, the tension between them finally boils over. Can they risk their friendship to take a chance on love? Or will fear keep them apart forever?

Book Three

On Call for You

He swore she was off-limits. She's ready to prove him wrong. Dr. Sophie Whitaker has spent her career proving herself in a world that underestimates her. As a brilliant but petite doctor, she's fought for respect every step of the way. Moving back to Anchor Bay is supposed to be a fresh start—not a temptation in the form of Lucas Carter. The rugged EMT with a cocky grin and a hero complex. The man her brother trusts with his life... and the one she should definitely stay away from. Lucas Carter lives by two rules: stay cool under pressure and never, ever cross the line with Sophie Whitaker. Even if she's gorgeous. Even if she's sharp-witted and impossible to ignore. Even if, after one stormy encounter stranded together, the idea of walking away feels damn near impossible. Now, every stolen glance and lingering touch has Lucas questioning everything—especially the rule that's kept him from going after the one woman he can't stop thinking about. Falling for Sophie could mean risking his oldest friendship. But walking away? That might be the biggest mistake of his life.

Book Four

Investigating Desire

A Slow-Burn Romantic Suspense with a Grumpy Detective and the Journalist Who Won't Back Down

Detective Nate Whitaker has sworn off love. After a messy divorce, he's buried himself in his work, content to keep his emotions locked away. But when a bold, relentless journalist starts shadowing him for an exclusive story, their push-and-pull dynamic ignites a slow burn neither of them can ignore.

Tessa Donovan has worked hard to make a name for herself. She's determined to crack open a case that's rocked this small town, even if it means getting under the skin of a brooding detective who wants nothing to do with her. But when her investigation stirs up danger, Nate has no choice but to keep her close. What starts as a reluctant partnership turns into something far more dangerous—a fiery attraction neither of them is ready for.

With a growing threat looming and tension crackling between them, this small-town romantic suspense is about to heat up. Can Nate and Tessa untangle the case before it's too late, or will their undeniable chemistry turn into the biggest risk of all?

Book Five

Falling for the Rescue

A Forced Proximity, Search and Rescue Romance Packed with Heat, Heart, and High Stakes Ryan Anderson thrives in the chaos of Search and Rescue, risking everything to save those in danger. He's fiercely independent, highly skilled, and never the one needing help—until a treacherous storm and a botched rescue mission leave him stranded, injured, and facing the one situation he can't control. Enter Sam Monroe—a tough, no-nonsense ex-military K9 handler who's spent years proving she doesn't need anyone. Haunted by her past and more comfortable in survival mode than emotional entanglements, Sam doesn't have time for distractions—especially not the kind with broad shoulders, smoldering intensity, and a stubborn streak to match her own. Forced to wait out the storm in a remote cabin in the wilderness, their reluctant alliance turns into something far more dangerous. Tensions ignite. Sparks fly. But neither of them is built for surrender—especially when old wounds and hidden vulnerabilities threaten to unravel the fragile trust between them. Will Sam and Ryan let down their walls and take a risk on love? Or will fear and pride keep them from the one person who finally sees them for who they truly are?

Hana York Books

♥

Hearts on Duty Series

Sparks of Temptation

Love's Anchor

On Call for You

Investigating Desire

Falling for the Rescue

A Heart Worth Mending

For a full list of titles, please visit Hana York's website

www.HanaYork.com

About the Author

H ana York writes fast-paced, heart-pounding contemporary romance packed with irresistible heroes, strong heroines, laugh-out-loud banter, and just the right amount of spice to keep things sizzling. Her books are for readers who love grumpy men falling hard, fierce women who don't need saving, and the kind of chemistry that sparks off the page.

When she's not crafting stories full of love, tension, and toe-curling moments, you'll find her daydreaming about small-town charm, plotting ridiculous meet-cutes, and consuming an unhealthy amount of coffee. She believes in happily-ever-afters, overprotective heroes who don't stand a chance against their heroines, and that every great love story should come with a side of sass.

If you love forced proximity, off-limits attraction, sizzling tension, and romance that makes your heart race, welcome to the world of Hana York!

Follow Hana York for new releases, exclusive content, and behind-the-scenes fun! www.HanaYork.com

Find all her books here: https://www.amazon.com/author/hanayork

Follow her on Instagram: https://www.instagram.com/hanayorkromance/

Follow her on Facebook: https://www.facebook.com/hanayorkromance/

Follow her on Good Reads: https://www.goodreads.com/author/show/54826946.Hana_York

Join her mailing list here: https://www.hanayork.com/subscribe

www.ingramcontent.com/pod-product-compliance
Lightning Source LLC
Chambersburg PA
CBHW071628140626
46555CB00021B/1247

9781967053117